NOOR JAHAN

GHIYAS BEG, A NOBLEMAN HAD TO FLEE WITH HIS FAMILY FROM PERSIA.

WHAT IS TO BECOME OF US?

DON'T WORRY. WITH THE RICHES WE HAVE MANAGED TO BRING AWAY, WE CAN MAKE A FRESH BEGINNING IN HINDUSTAN.

SUDDENLY —
DON'T MOVE.
SURRENDER EVERYTHING IF YOU VALUE YOUR LIVES.
RELIEVING GHIYAS BEG OF HIS RICHES, HIS PROVISIONS AND HIS MULES, THE DACOITS RODE AWAY.

GHIYAS AND HIS FAMILY HAD TO TREK ACROSS THE DESERT. SOON—
MOTHER, I'M HUNGRY.
FATHER, GET US SOMETHING TO EAT.
WITH WHAT SHALL I FEED THE HUNGRY CHILDREN? EMPTY WORDS?

JUST THEN, OVERCOME BY HUNGER AND FATIGUE, GHIYAS BEG'S PREGNANT WIFE FAINTED. . .

. . . AND GAVE BIRTH TO A DAUGHTER.
YA ALLAH!* WHY THIS UNTIMELY GIFT?

* O GOD

BEGUM, WHEN WE CAN'T FEED THREE CHILDREN, HOW WILL WE FEED ONE MORE? WE'D BETTER LEAVE THIS CHILD HERE.
OH NO! IF WE DESERT THE BABY, ALLAH WILL NEVER FORGIVE US.

HE IS ALL-KNOWING. HE WILL UNDER-STAND. HE WON'T BE ANGRY WITH US.

FINALLY, GHIYAS BEG PREVAILED UPON HIS WIFE TO LEAVE THE CHILD BEHIND.
MY DARLING, FORGIVE US.
DON'T GRIEVE. ALLAH WILL PROTECT HER.

A FEW HOURS LATER, MASUD KHAN, A WEALTHY TRADER, HAPPENED TO PASS BY.
A CHILD'S CRY— IN THIS TERRIBLE JUNGLE!
WAH... WAH...

WHAT A LOVELY CHILD! I WILL TRACK DOWN THE BEASTS RESPONSIBLE FOR THIS AND HAVE THEM PUNISHED.

GHIYAS BEG AND HIS FAMILY WERE SOON OVERTAKEN BY MASUD KHAN'S CARAVAN.
THIS CHILD IS CRYING FOR ITS HEARTLESS MOTHER. WHAT SHALL WE DO?
WAH... WAH...
MY BABY!

DON'T CRY! I AM COMING!

THE CHILD HAS CALMED DOWN. SHE MUST BE THE MOTHER.

THOUGH WE LEFT THE CHILD BEHIND, SHE HAS BEEN SENT BACK TO US. IT MUST BE THE WILL OF ALLAH THAT WE KEEP HER.
SO YOU ARE THE MONSTROUS BRUTES WHO ABANDONED THAT HELPLESS BABY!

SIR, YOU WILL NOT THINK SO WHEN YOU HAVE HEARD OUR STORY.

WHEN GHIYAS BEG CONCLUDED HIS TALE—
BROTHER, PARDON ME FOR JUDGING YOU.
WE ARE GRATEFUL TO YOU, SIR, FOR GIVING US BACK OUR BABY.

IT IS ALLAH YOU SHOULD BE GRATEFUL TO!
SINCE WE GOT HER BACK BY ALLAH'S MERCY, WE SHALL CALL HER MEHER.

* AN OFFICIAL ⊗ REFUGE OF THE UNIVERSE

ON ONE SUCH OCCASION —

WHAT A LOVELY, CHARMING, GRACEFUL CHILD! I WONDER WHOSE DAUGHTER SHE IS.

WHO ARE YOU, LITTLE GIRL?

WHO COULD THAT BE? HE'S COMING THIS WAY. I'LL ASK HIM.

HOW DO YOU KNOW?
HOW DARE YOU QUESTION THE WORDS OF SALIM, THE EMPEROR'S SON?

AT THAT MOMENT, MEHER'S MOTHER RETURNED.
IF MY DAUGHTER HAS BEEN NAUGHTY, I BEG YOU TO PARDON HER, JAHANPANAH.
SHE IS A BRIGHT CHILD. LET HER COME HERE EVERY DAY AND PLAY WITH SALIM.

ONE DAY, WHEN AKBAR WAS RELAXING IN THE GARDEN, MEHER CAME RUNNING UP.
ABBAJAN, SALIM IS ANGRY. PROTECT ME.
WHAT MADE HIM ANGRY, DEAR?

BEFORE SHE COULD REPLY —
DON'T HIDE BEHIND ABBAJAN. COME OUT, YOU COWARD.
NO, I WON'T.

SALIM, WHY ARE YOU ANGRY WITH THE POOR DARLING?
POOR DARLING! SHE IS A LITTLE DEVIL.

YOU KNOW HOW MUCH I LOVE MY DOVES. TODAY, WHEN I WAS FONDLING THEM, I WAS CALLED AWAY.

"I ENTRUSTED THE TWO DOVES TO MEHER."
MEHER, PLEASE TAKE CARE OF THEM. I WILL BE BACK SOON.
DON'T WORRY. TAKE YOUR OWN TIME.

"AFTER A WHILE, WHEN I RETURNED, I WAS SURPRISED TO SEE ONLY ONE DOVE WITH HER."
WHERE'S THE OTHER ONE?
IT FLEW AWAY.

"I WAS ENRAGED BY HER ATTITUDE AND HER CALM REPLY."

HOW DID IT HAPPEN?

. . . AND ARCHERY.
THAT WAS A GOOD SHOT, MEHER!

YEARS ROLLED BY. ONE DAY—
MEHER, I LOVE YOU. WILL YOU MARRY ME?

BUT HOW CAN I? YOU ARE A PRINCE. I AM . . .
. . . AN ANGEL! LIGHT OF THE WORLD— OF MY WORLD!

SALIM'S LOVE FOR MEHER SOON BEGAN TO BE TALKED ABOUT.
WILL SALIM MARRY HER?
WILL THE EMPEROR GIVE HIS CONSENT?

THE NEWS REACHED AKBAR'S EARS.
IT CAN'T BE TRUE. SALIM IS A RESPON-SIBLE BOY.

PERTURBED, AKBAR WALKED OUT INTO THE GARDEN.

SUDDENLY, HE HEARD VOICES.
SALIM!
MY LOVE!

MEHER, I MAY GIVE UP THE THRONE BUT NOT YOU. YOU WILL SOON BE MY WIFE.
SO WHAT I HEARD IS TRUE.

THE DAUGHTER OF A REFUGEE TO MARRY THE CROWN PRINCE! NEVER! I MUST SEPARATE THEM.

THE NEXT DAY, THE EMPEROR SENT FOR HIS SON.
SALIM, I WANT YOU TO LEAD AN EXPEDITION TO THE DECCAN.
YOU ARE CONFERRING A GREAT HONOUR ON ME, JAHANPANAH.

ON THE EVE OF HIS DEPARTURE, MEHER PRESENTED SALIM WITH AN EMBROIDERED HANDKERCHIEF.
MAY THOSE ROSEBUDS ALWAYS REMIND YOU OF ME.

DON'T WORRY, MEHER. I WILL BE BACK SOON.
OH, SALIM!
WHILE TAKING CARE TO FULFIL MY DUTIES AS AN EMPEROR, HAVE I FAILED AS A FATHER?

ONE DAY, SOON AFTER SALIM HAD LEFT, AKBAR TOOK MEHER TO THE SHRINE OF SAINT CHISHTI.
I PRAYED TO CHISHTI AND GOT SALIM. I PRAYED, NOT FOR A SON; BUT FOR THE FUTURE EMPEROR.

REMEMBER, MEHER. SALIM DOES NOT BELONG TO ME OR TO ANYONE. HE BELONGS TO THE EMPIRE.
I UNDERSTAND, ABBAJAN. I GIVE YOU MY WORD THAT I WILL NOT COME BETWEEN SALIM AND THE EMPIRE.

AS MEHER RODE OUT ONE MORNING TO EXERCISE HER HORSE —
A RUNAWAY HORSE! THE WOMAN SEEMS TO BE IN DISTRESS! I MUST SAVE HER!

I MUST STOP THE HORSE BEFORE SHE IS TOSSED OFF ITS BACK.

THE YOUNG RIDER WAS SHER AFGHAN, AN OFFICER IN THE IMPERIAL ARMY.
HOW DARE YOU HOLD THE REINS OF MY HORSE?
I THOUGHT YOU WERE IN TROUBLE.

INDEED! NONE IN AGRA HAS FOUND IT NECESSARY TO COME TO MY AID WHILE I AM ON HORSEBACK.

A PROUD WOMAN INDEED! BUT BRAVE AND BEAUTIFUL.

LATER IN THE DAY, SHER AFGHAN CALLED ON THE EMPEROR AND PRESENTED HIM WITH A TIGER.

SHER AFGHAN, YOUR GIFTS ARE ALWAYS REFRESHINGLY DIFFERENT FROM THE USUAL GIFTS OTHERS BRING.

JAHANPANAH, I AM GLAD THAT MY MODEST GIFT HAS PLEASED YOU.

WHY! IF IT ISN'T THE STRANGER I MET IN THE MORNING!

SUDDENLY, A STRONG GUST OF WIND SWEPT MEHER'S VEIL OFF HER SHOULDERS.

YOU RISKED YOUR LIFE FOR MY VEIL! WHY?

SHER, YOU ARE AS FEARLESS AS A TIGER ASK FOR ANYTHING; YOU WILL HAVE IT.
JAHANPANAH! I WANT THE OWNER OF THE VEIL FOR A WIFE.
NO!

SHE IS THE DAUGHTER OF GHIYAS BEG. HOW CAN I GIVE HER AWAY?
BUT YOU HAVE PROMISED TO GIVE ME ANYTHING I ASK FOR, JAHANPANAH!

WHEN AKBAR TURNED HELPLESSLY TO MEHER—
FORGIVE ME, SALIM.
I WILL ABIDE BY YOUR WISHES, ABBAJAN. YOU HAVE BEEN MORE THAN A FATHER TO ME.

AFTER THE WEDDING, MEHER WENT WITH HER HUSBAND TO BURDWAN, WHERE SHE LED A HAPPY LIFE. SHE OFTEN WENT OUT RIDING AND HUNTING WITH HIM.
YOU ARE A GOOD SHOT AND AN EXCELLENT RIDER, MEHER. TELL ME, WHO TRAINED YOU?
I LEARNT BOTH SHOOTING AND RIDING WHEN I WAS VERY YOUNG.
OH, SALIM!

IN DUE COURSE, MEHER BECAME THE PROUD MOTHER OF A BEAUTIFUL GIRL WHOM SHE CALLED LADLI.

ONE DAY, AS MEHER AND SHER AFGHAN WERE PLAYING CHESS...

...A MESSENGER CAME WITH BAD NEWS.
MY LORD, EMPEROR AKBAR IS DEAD.
ABBAJAN!
MEHER!

LATER—
I HEAR, SALIM HAS ASSUMED THE TITLE— JAHANGIR — AND SUCCEEDED HIS FATHER AS THE EMPEROR.
YES. WE SHOULD CALL ON THE NEW EMPEROR WITH GIFTS.

MEHER, HOWEVER, WAS RELUCTANT TO VISIT AGRA.
MUST WE GO TO AGRA? CAN'T WE SEND THE GIFTS WITH AN OFFICER...
NO. I WANT TO SEE THE EMPEROR PERSONALLY. HE IS MY BENEFACTOR.

WHEN I WAS IN HIS SERVICE, IT WAS HE WHO HAILED ME AS SHER FOR KILLING A TIGER.

* AN ORIENTAL PERFUME

* FAMILY BAZAAR HELD ONCE A YEAR, AT THE PALACE.

LATER, IN THE PALACE GARDEN—
MEHER, MARRY ME AND BE MY QUEEN.
I CAN'T, JAHANPANAH.

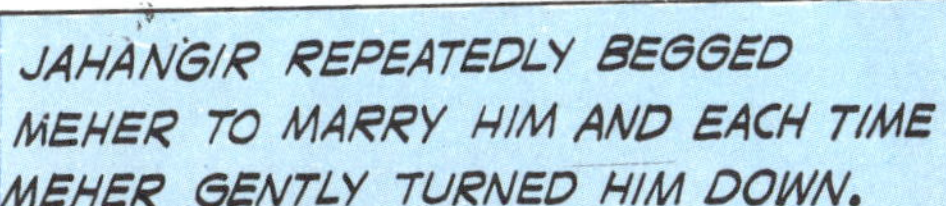
JAHANGIR REPEATEDLY BEGGED MEHER TO MARRY HIM AND EACH TIME MEHER GENTLY TURNED HIM DOWN.

THE SPRING OF HER LOVE FOR ME HAS DRIED UP.

HOW CAN I MARRY HIM? I MUST KEEP MY PROMISE TO ABBAJAN.

THEN ONE DAY, SHE OVERHEARD SOME COURTIERS TALKING.
THE EMPEROR IS PINING FOR GHIYAS BEG'S DAUGHTER.
MATTERS OF STATE ARE BEING NEGLECTED.

* SUPERINTENDENT OF THE ROYAL HOUSEHOLD.

IT IS TO SAVE THE EMPIRE THAT I AM ASKING YOU TO MARRY THE EMPEROR.

ASSUMING THE NEW NAME NOOR JAHAN—MEHER MARRIED JAHANGIR. SHE TOOK A KEEN INTEREST IN THE ADMINISTRATION OF THE STATE.
JAHANPANAH, THE PLIGHT OF THE ORPHANS IS HEART-RENDING.
WHAT CAN WE DO ABOUT IT, NOOR?

WHY CAN'T WE BRING UP THE ORPHANS? TO WHOM ELSE CAN THEY TURN?
ALL RIGHT. LET US ISSUE A PROCLAMATION IN YOUR NAME, OFFERING OUR PROTECTION TO THE ORPHANS.

NOT IN MY NAME, JAHANPANAH!
WHY NOT, NOOR? IT IS YOUR IDEA. THE PROCLAMATION SHOULD BEAR YOUR SIGNATURE.

AND IN FUTURE YOU MAY ISSUE ANY PROCLAMATION ON YOUR OWN.

NOOR JAHAN WON THE ADMIRATION OF THE PEOPLE TOO.
SHE IS KIND AND GENEROUS. SHE TAKES GOOD CARE OF THE ORPHANS.
SHE EVEN ARRANGES THEIR MARRIAGES.

BUT THERE WERE SOME WHO RESENTED NOOR JAHAN'S INFLUENCE OVER JAHANGIR. PROMINENT AMONG THEM WAS MAHABAT KHAN.
MAHABAT KHAN, SHE HAS NOW BEGUN TO RECEIVE COURTIERS AND DISCUSS STATE ISSUES.
OUR EMPEROR DANCES TO HER TUNE.

WHEN NOOR JAHAN GOT LADLI MARRIED TO SHAHRIYAR, JAHANGIR'S FOURTH SON BY AN EARLIER MARRIAGE —
NOW SHE WILL GET THE EMPEROR TO DECLARE SHAHRIYAR AS HIS SUCCESSOR
THAT WOULD BE UNFAIR TO THE ELDER PRINCE, KHURRAM.

NOOR JAHAN WAS NOT UNAWARE OF MAHABAT KHAN'S HOSTILITY.
JAHANPANAH, I DO NOT TRUST MAHABAT KHAN.
I'M AFRAID I DON'T SHARE YOUR APPREHENSION, MY DEAR.

DON'T FORGET THAT IT WAS HE WHO PUT DOWN THE REBELLION OF PRINCE KHURRAM.
BUT HE IS CORRUPT. HAS HE EVER SUBMITTED THE ACCOUNTS OF THE VARIOUS EXPEDITIONS HE HAS LED?

ALL RIGHT, MY DEAR. I WILL SUMMON HIM FROM THE DECCAN, AND QUESTION HIM. BUT LET THIS NOT DISTURB OUR PLANS TO VISIT KABUL.
JAHANPANAH, I LOOK FORWARD TO THE TRIP.

ON THEIR WAY TO KABUL, JAHANGIR AND NOOR JAHAN CAMPED WITH THE ROYAL ARMY ON THE BANK OF THE RIVER JHELUM.
JAHANPANAH, I HEAR THAT MAHABAT KHAN WILL BE MEETING YOU.
YES, HE IS EXPECTED ANY DAY NOW.

THE NEXT DAY THE EMPEROR AND HIS RETINUE HAD TO CROSS THE RIVER.
JAHANPANAH, I WILL GO ACROSS FIRST AND MAKE ARRANGEMENTS FOR YOUR STAY.
YOU ARE ALWAYS CONCERNED ABOUT MY COMFORT, NOOR.

LEAVING THE EMPEROR BEHIND WITH A SMALL PARTY OF MEN, NOOR JAHAN CROSSED THE RIVER WITH THE ARMY. A BRIDGE OF BOATS HAD BEEN SPECIALLY LAID FOR THE PURPOSE.

ALL ARRANGEMENTS WERE MADE FOR HIS STAY BUT THE EMPEROR DID NOT TURN UP.
WHY HASN'T HE COME AS YET?

SHE SOON LEARNT WHY.
BEGUM SAHIBA, MAHABAT KHAN'S ARMY HAS SURROUNDED THE EMPEROR'S PARTY.
WHAT!

WE SHOULD RUSH TO HIS RESCUE! WE WILL CROSS THE RIVER.
BUT BEGUM SAHIBA, THE ENEMY HAVE TAKEN THE BRIDGE!

BRIDGE OR NO BRIDGE, WE SHALL CROSS THE RIVER! NOW DO AS I SAY.

SHE MOUNTED AN ELEPHANT AND TAKING WITH HER A SMALL SECTION OF THE ARMY, CROSSED THE RIVER WHICH WAS IN SPATE.

IN THE FIGHT THAT FOLLOWED, SHE WAS DEFEATED AND TAKEN CAPTIVE.
BEGUM SAHIBA, WHY DID YOU TAKE THIS UNNECESSARY RISK?
I HAVE NO WISH TO SPEAK TO A TRAITOR. LEAD ME TO THE EMPEROR.

NOOR, YOU ARE SAFE! WHAT A RELIEF!
JAHANPANAH, WE HAVE NO TIME TO WASTE. TELL MAHABAT KHAN THAT YOU WOULD LIKE TO INSPECT THE ARMY.

CONFIDENT OF HIS POSITION, MAHABAT KHAN SAW NO HARM IN ACCEDING TO THE EMPEROR'S REQUEST.
LONG LIVE THE EMPEROR!

AS PREPLANNED, THE SECTION OF THE ARMY LEFT BEHIND BY NOOR JAHAN, CROSSED THE RIVER AND TOOK THE ENEMY BY SURPRISE.

IN THE BATTLE THAT FOLLOWED, JAHANGIR'S ARMY WON.
NOOR, I OWE MY LIFE AS WELL AS MY HONOUR TO YOU.
JAHANGIR DID NOT LIVE LONG AFTER THESE EVENTS. ON HIS DEATH, NOOR JAHAN SETTLED IN LAHORE WHERE SHE DEVOTED THE REST OF HER LIFE TO THE MAKING OF PERFUME.